For my Mama, who always tucked me in tight.
And for my Papa, a true dreamer. - A.B.H.

To my daughter, Emily, who has filled my life with light. -G.C.

Text copyright © 2005 by Ashley Brooke Hornsby
Illustrations © 2005 by Greg Couch

Glo E ™ is a trademark of Cepia LLC.

A CEPIA LLC BOOK

Published in the United States of America by Cepia LLC.,
Saint Louis, Missouri – www.glo-e.com

ISBN 0-9777241-1-5

PRINTED IN CHINA

Pretty Little Lilly
and the
Magical Night

Written by:
Ashley Hornsby

Illustrated by:
Greg Couch

This isn't a sad or scary story, as you'll soon see, but one of wonder and magic and how important a wish and a dream can be. This story begins on a magical shooting star night, and takes us to a place of dreamlike light.

Pretty Little Lilly, a girl from
a land not so far away, was
getting ready for bed like she
did every day. She crawled into
her soft snuggly bed. Her mama
walked into her room and gave
her a kiss on the head.

She pulled up the blankets and
tucked her in tight, hoping her
sweet little girl would not cry
tonight. "Sweet dreams, my Pretty
Little Lilly, I love you, good night."
Lilly's eyes filled with tears and
she gave a small sigh, "I love you
too Mama," and then she started
to cry.

Now Lilly and her mother did
this routine every night, and Lilly
always cried when her mom
turned out the light.

But tonight was different, as these
magical nights are; Lilly's mom looked
out the window and saw a shooting
star! Hundreds and hundreds of bright
shining stars were shooting through
the sky! It was a beautiful sight,
I would not tell a lie.

"Lilly, look!" her mother said, "Hurry,
make a wish!" Lilly jumped out of bed
and closed her eyes tight, "I wish I
would not be afraid of the dark,
I wish for light!"

"Mama, what if my wish doesn't come true?" Her mother hugged her and smiled, "My sweet little Lilly, it will for you. Wishes come true, and they start in your dreams, no matter how big or small your sweet wish seems."

Her mom turned out the light and cracked the door, "Mama, could you please open it a little bit more?" And with that Pretty Little Lilly was left alone in the night…

...All alone with a small
crack of light.

As Lilly drifted off to sleep,
something magical began to happen,
something that doesn't happen too often. Her
room began to fill with light, and as the light
swirled and twirled it was a breathtaking sight!
Shades of pink, blue, yellow and green, this was
a sight only true dreamers have seen.

You would never believe it, but trust me it's
true, a little glowing bear appeared right out of
the blue!

The sweet little bear snuggled up close and
snuggled up tight, "Pretty Little Lilly, are you
the one who wished for light?" As the sweet
little bear whispered in her ear, Lilly awoke
to the words she was dreaming to hear.
"Who…who are you?" Although in her
heart, she secretly knew.

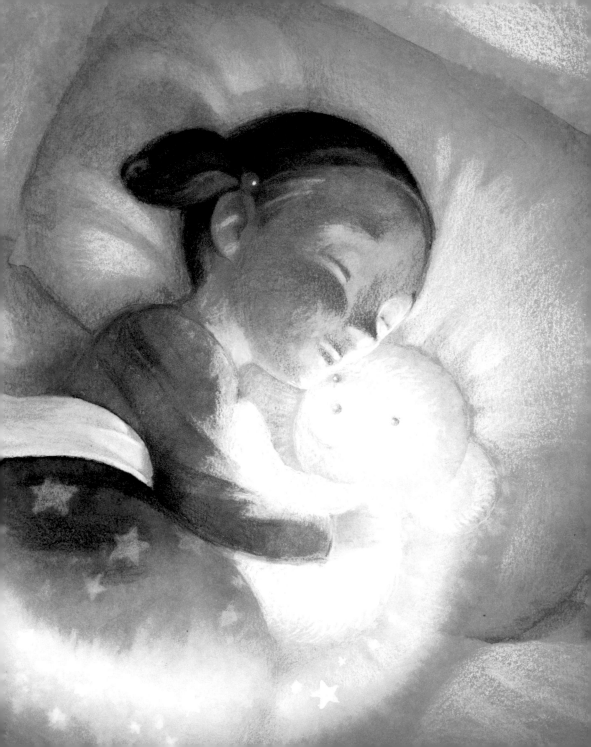

"You wished upon a shooting star, and your sweet little wish traveled far, and swirled and twirled and danced and dreamed and brought me to your little world, so it would seem. I'm Glo E and I'll help you through the night, take my paw and hold on tight!"

Pretty Little Lilly took a deep breath and held out her hand, and in one magical beautiful second she was swept off to a different land.

This land was called Northern Lights, a land of love, a land of light, a land of not one tiny little fright. There were hundreds of bears and hundreds of puppies. They all lit up, and you should have seen the monkeys! Glo E explained how this place came to be, he explained it with excitement and glee! It grew from the wishes of sweet little kids, who had the same feelings, just like Lilly did. Little boys and girls who were afraid of the night, who wished and dreamed for a magical light.

They traveled through this dreamlike land, and all the while Glo E held her little hand. They crossed a colorful river of lights, the colors swirled and twirled and rippled with delight. Then they climbed a mountain higher than the sky and watched as stars and moonbeams quickly sparkled by.

At the top of the
mountain, Lilly couldn't
believe her eyes; the most
beautiful castle was very nearby. The
towers lit up with a glistening glow
and to Lilly's excitement it
started to snow!

The snowflakes were sparkling and
twinkling with light. There had never
been a more spectacular night. Pretty
Little Lilly looked up with those
sweet little eyes, and it was at this
point in time that she got
a surprise.

A beautiful princess with long flowing hair told Lilly that she had a sweet and magical story to share. "A long time ago, far far away, I was a child who cried at the end of the day. I was afraid of the dark, afraid of the night, afraid that everything would not be all right. I would cry till there were no more tears, and then I was left alone with all my fears. I realized one day that this just wasn't right…there really isn't anything wrong with the night.

Night is for magic, starlight, moonbeams; Night is for soft colorful dreams. Colors so vibrant that glisten and glow, nighttime is special and I thought you should know. But now it's time for you to go back to your soft snuggly bed." Lilly replied, " I would rather just stay here instead."

The princess gave a sweet smile as she looked at the child, "Pretty Little Lilly this is the place where your dreams can run wild. At the end of the day, when your mama turns out the light, this is where your dreams will bring you when it is night."

"All you have to do is give Glo E your hand, and then he will bring you to our magical land. But for now it's time to go back to your bed, your mother would miss you if you stayed here instead."

Then once again, as it happened
before, the colors of light swirled and
twirled and Lilly knew at this moment
she was leaving their world.

As quick as she got there, she was
back in her room, and surprisingly
Lilly was sad to not see the moon.

"Good morning my Pretty Little Lilly!" her mother walked in, and noticed the soft little bear snuggled next to Lilly's chin. "What a cute little bear!"

It was at this point in time, Lilly had the sweet and magical story to share.